HANNA SCHROY

strange and amazing

inquiry@ironcircus.com www.ironcircus.com

Writer/Artist
Hanna Schroy

Publisher
C. Spike Trotman

Editor
Andrea Purcell

Art Director/Cover Design
Matt Sheridan

Print Technician/Book Design
Beth Scorzato

Proofreader
Abby Lehrke

Published by
Iron Circus Comics
329 West 18th Street, Suite 604
Chicago, IL 60616
ironcircus.com

First Edition: November 2020

ISBN: 978-1-945820-72-4

10 9 8 7 6 5 4 3 2 1

printed in China

Last Dance

Publisher's Cataloging-In-Publication Data
(Prepared by The Donohue Group, Inc.)

Names: Schroy, Hanna, author, illustrator. | Spike, 1978- publisher. | Purcell, Andrea, editor. | Sheridan, Matt, 1978- designer. | Scorzato, Beth, designer.
Title: Last dance / writer/artist, Hanna Schroy ; publisher, C. Spike Trotman ; editor, Andrea Purcell ; art director/cover design, Matt Sheridan ; print technician/book design, Beth Scorzato ; proofreader, Abby Lehrke.
Description: First edition. | Chicago, IL : Iron Circus Comics, 2020. | Interest age level: 008-012. | Summary: "An injured dancer uses the aid of a dark spirit to regain her title as prima ballerina, but it comes with a great personal cost"–Provided by publisher.
Identifiers: ISBN 9781945820724
Subjects: LCSH: Ballerinas–Comic books, strips, etc. | Dancing injuries–Comic books, strips, etc. | Spirits-Comic books, strips, etc. | CYAC: Ballerinas–Fiction. | Dancing injuries–Fiction. | Spirits–Fiction. | LCGFT: Graphic novels.
Classification: LCC PZ7.7.S378 La 2020 | DDC 741.5973 [Fic]–dc23

1

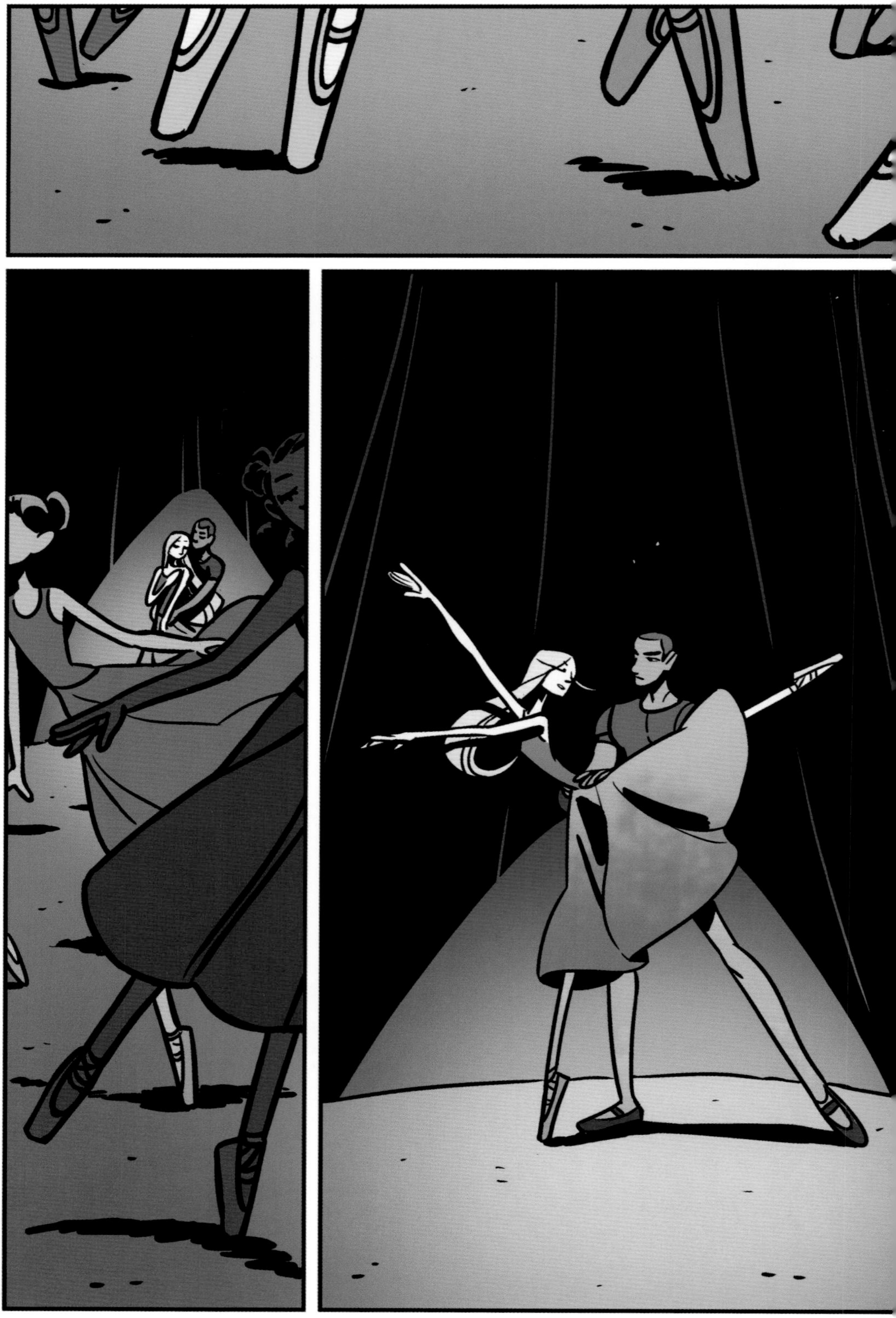

WATCH YOUR ANGLES!

KEEP YOUR ARMS LIGHT!
DON'T FORGET YOUR BACK FOOT!
STOP! STOP! STOP!

NICOLAS, MIRIAM!

NICOLAS, MAKE SURE YOU'RE WATCHING MIRIAM.
AND MIRIAM, DON'T RUSH INTO THAT LEAP.

YOU NEED TO GLIDE INTO IT.
REMEMBER, THIS IS YOUR PAS DE DEUX, THE DANCE OF TWO—
— IT SHOULD BE A TENDER MOMENT.
YES, ALEXANDRE, SIR.

AGAIN, FROM THE PAS DE BOURRÉE!

WHAT WAS THAT?
YOU TREAD LIKE A BULL.
I DO NOT!

I'VE SEEN THE EXTRA HOURS YOU PULL.
YOU'RE OVER – WORKING YOURSELF. IT'S MAKING YOU SLOPPY.

LORELEI ON THE OTHER HAND...
SHE ONLY JOINED OUR COMPANY A MONTH AGO AND SHE'S ALREADY IMPROVED CONSIDERABLY.
YOU SLIP UP AND I'LL BE DANCING THE PAS DE DEUX WITH *HER* INSTEAD.

OH, DON'T BE UNGRATEFUL, NICOLAS.
YOU KNOW I'M STILL THE BEST DANCER HERE.

AND, PLACES!
SHE COULD NEVER TAKE THIS ROLE AS SERIOUSLY AS I DO.

KEEP THAT LEG STRAIGHT!

WHAT WAS THAT?
ARE YOU OK?
WATCH YOUR
TURN OUT!
IT'S NOTHING,
KEEP GOING.
REMEMBER WHAT WE
TALKED ABOUT, PERFECT
YOUR CHASSÉ!

CRACK!
MIRIAM?
AAAH!
MIRIAM!

WHAT HAPPENED?
I'M NOT SURE. I THINK SHE MUST HAVE PULLED SOMETHING.
SUZANNE!
YES, SIR?
CALL AN AMBULANCE.
TELL THEM SOMEONE'S BEEN INJURED.

EMERGENCY
ST. SERVATIUS GENERAL HOSPITAL
MIRIAM, IS IT?
YES, DOCTOR.

WELL, MIRIAM, I'VE GOT SOME GOOD NEWS AND SOME BAD NEWS.

GOOD NEWS IS YOUR LEG WILL RECOVER.

WITH A FEW SESSIONS OF PHYSICAL THERAPY YOU WILL BE BACK ON YOUR FEET IN NO TIME.
THAT'S GOOD TO HEAR.

IT MAY BE A WHILE, BUT YOU SHOULDN'T NOTICE ANY MAJOR CHANGES IN YOUR WALK.

DR. BAKSHI,
I NEED TO KNOW...
WHEN WILL
I BE ABLE TO
DANCE AGAIN?

MIRIAM, THERE'S
SOMETHING YOU NEED
TO UNDERSTAND.

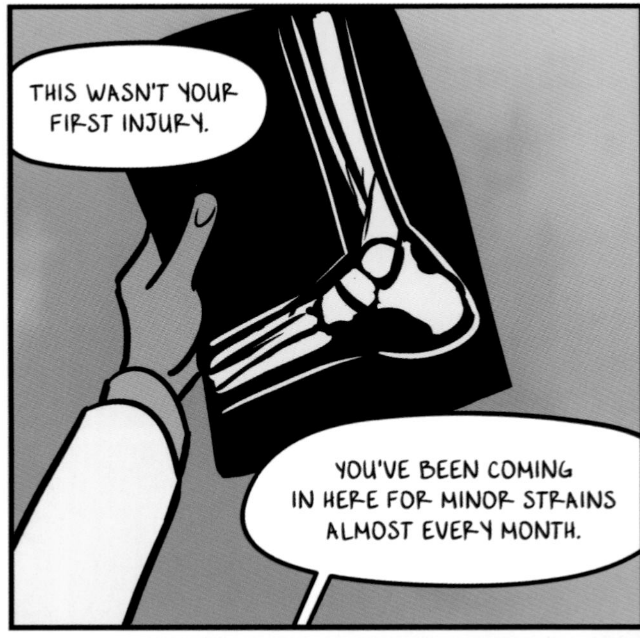
THIS WASN'T YOUR
FIRST INJURY.
YOU'VE BEEN COMING
IN HERE FOR MINOR STRAINS
ALMOST EVERY MONTH.

HONESTLY, I'M
SURPRISED YOU DIDN'T BREAK
SOMETHING SOONER.

MIRIAM, IF YOU
WANT MY PROFESSIONAL
OPINION...

YOU SHOULD FORGET ABOUT RETURNING TO DANCING.
WHAT?

IF YOU LOOK AT THE FRACTURE HERE—
— THERE'S A MULTITUDE OF OTHER HAIRLINE FRACTURES SURROUNDING...

ON TOP OF THE LOSS OF CARTILAGE...

I BELIEVE YOU SHOULD FOCUS INSTEAD ON REGAINING YOUR ABILITY TO WALK FREELY.

DR. BAKSHI, YOU DON'T UNDERSTAND!
DANCING IS MY LIFE! I CAN'T JUST GIVE IT UP.
I'M SORRY, MIRIAM, BUT YOU'VE ALREADY DONE ENOUGH HARM TO YOUR BODY.
WITH ENOUGH PHYSICAL THERAPY, I BELIEVE YOU CAN WALK AGAIN WITHOUT A LIMP.

I WILL LEAVE YOU TWO ALONE TO PROCESS THE NEWS.
A NURSE WILL COME IN LATER TO FIT YOU WITH A BOOT.

CLICK

WELL...
IT COULD BE WORSE?

HOW, NICOLAS?
I'VE JUST LOST EVERYTHING!

DON'T BE DRAMATIC.
YOU'RE ALIVE, RIGHT? YOU STILL HAVE YOUR FRIENDS, YOUR FAMILY.
THERE'S STILL A LOT YOU CAN DO.

NICOLAS, YOU DON'T UNDERSTAND.
EVER SINCE I WAS A LITTLE GIRL, DANCING IS ALL I'VE EVER WANTED.

IT'S ALL I'VE EVER BEEN ANY GOOD AT.
I'VE WORKED SO HARD TO GET WHERE I AM, THEN ONE STUPID MISTAKE...

MAYBE THE DOCTOR WAS WRONG?

PEOPLE RECOVER FROM NJURIES ALL THE TIME!
NO, MIRIAM. DR. BAKSHI SAID IT WAS SERIOUS.

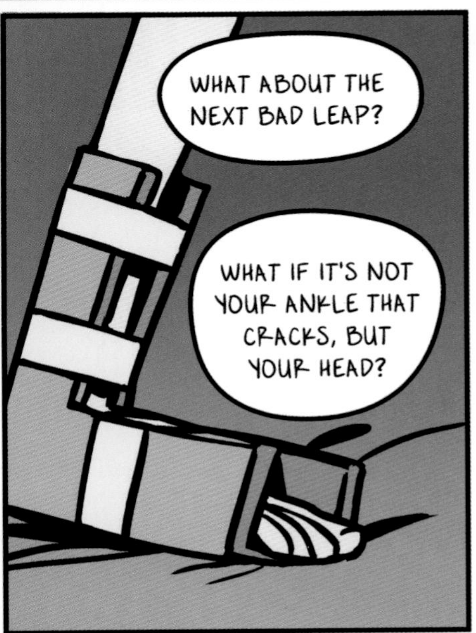
WHAT ABOUT THE NEXT BAD LEAP?
WHAT IF IT'S NOT YOUR ANKLE THAT CRACKS, BUT YOUR HEAD?

I CAN'T JUST GIVE UP!
WHY NOT?

ACCEPT IT, MIRIAM, NOT EVERYONE'S CUT OUT TO GO PROFESSIONAL.
MAYBE IT'S TIME TO TRY SOMETHING ELSE.

NICOLAS, I THINK YOU SHOULD LEAVE.

MIRIAM, I—
GO, NICOLAS.

FINE.

I'LL COME BACK WHEN YOU'RE READY TO LEAVE.

GRRP

AH, MIRIAM!

I SEE YOU'VE RETURNED. WHAT DID THE DOCTORS HAVE TO SAY?
OH, NOT MUCH...

THEY JUST SAID I NEED A FEW DAYS' REST AND I'LL BE RIGHT AS RAIN!

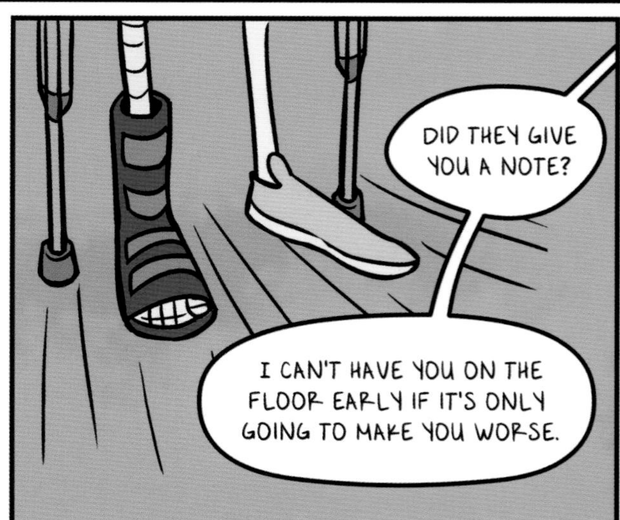
DID THEY GIVE YOU A NOTE?
I CAN'T HAVE YOU ON THE FLOOR EARLY IF IT'S ONLY GOING TO MAKE YOU WORSE.

NOT EXACTLY...

MIRIAM, I THINK IT'S FOR THE BEST THAT YOU SIT OUT THEN—

— FOR THE FORESEEABLE FUTURE.
WHAT?

BUT, SIR! JUST GIVE ME A DAY OR TWO, I'M SURE I'LL BE FINE!
MIRIAM.

LOOK AT YOURSELF!
HOW CAN YOU EXPECT TO DANCE LIKE THIS?

SIR, I CAN DO IT! PLEASE, JUST LET ME TRY.

FINE, THEN. SHOW ME A RELEVÉ.

TAKE A SEAT,
MIRIAM.

HI, MIRIAM, IS IT?
DO YOU MIND IF WE SIT HERE?
SURE, DO WHAT YOU WANT.
I'M DANIEL—
— AND THIS IS SUZANNE.

WE SAW WHAT HAPPENED. THAT LOOKED ROUGH.
YEAH, ALEXANDRE SHOULDN'T HAVE ASKED YOU TO DO THAT.

HONESTLY, I'M SURPRISED YOU EVEN MADE IT OUT OF THE HOSPITAL SO SOON.

YOU KNOW, I WAS THERE WHEN YOU FELL.
IT WAS JUST AWFUL!
YEAH, WELL, I'M FINE NOW.

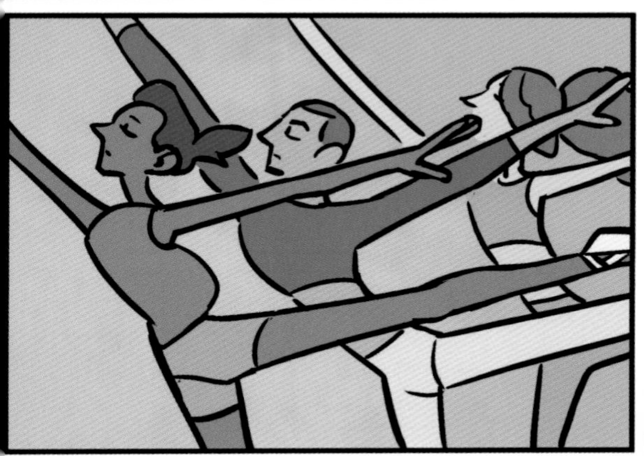

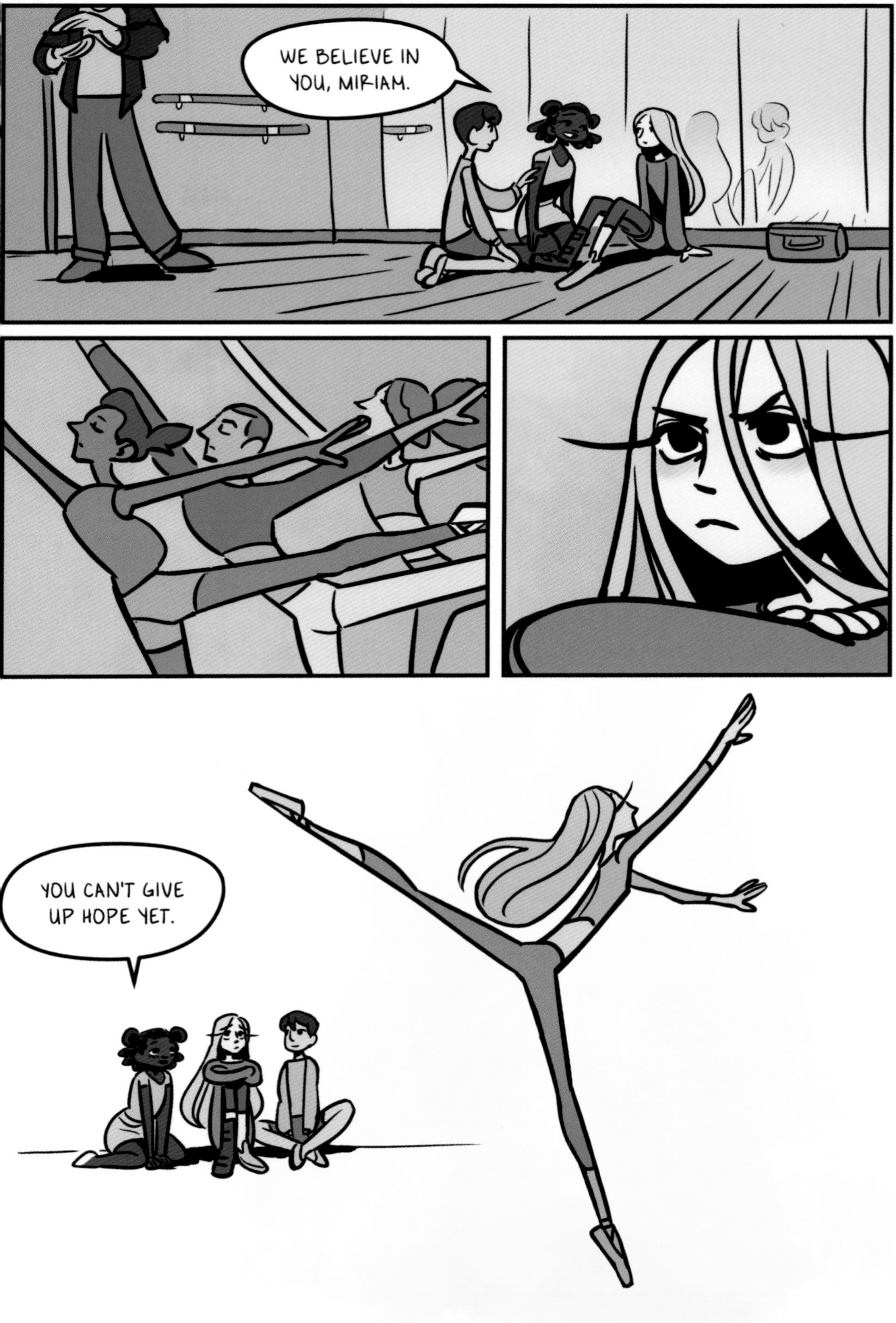

YOU CAN'T GIVE
UP HOPE YET.

2

PRACTICE STARTS AT NINE A.M. TOMORROW, DON'T BE LATE!

HOW ARE YOU FEELING?
I'M FINE.

TODAY MUST HAVE BEEN HARD ON YOU.

WE WERE WONDERING IF YOU'D LIKE TO GO OUT FOR COFFEE WITH US?
OUR TREAT.

THANK YOU, BUT MAYBE NEXT TIME.

I'VE GOT SOMETHING I NEED TO DEAL WITH FIRST.

NICOLAS!

WHAT DID YOU SAY TO ALEXANDRE?

MIRIAM, CALM DOWN. I ONLY TOLD HIM THE TRUTH.
WHAT, THAT I'M USELESS? THAT I CAN'T DANCE?

YOU SHOULD HAVE JUST STAYED OUT OF THIS, I WAS HANDLING IT FINE.
BY, WHAT, *LYING* TO THE INSTRUCTOR?

I ONLY TOLD HIM WHAT THE DOCTOR SAID.

AND I DON'T REGRET IT.

PUSHING YOURSELF TOO HARD IS WHAT GOT YOU IN THIS SITUATION IN THE FIRST PLACE.

I WON'T LET THIS COMPANY SUFFER BECAUSE YOU DON'T KNOW HOW TO ACCEPT YOUR OWN LIMITS.

KEEP COMING TO PRACTICE FOR ALL I CARE.
BUT I WON'T LET YOU TAKE THIS BALLET DOWN WITH YOU.

ROMEO
and
JULIET
STAR
AWARD
FIRST

FWUMP

MOMMY, I DID IT! I LANDED MY LEAP!
YES, HONEY, YOU DID.
BUT YOU BENT YOUR BACK LEG. THE JUDGES AREN'T GOING TO LIKE THAT.
SORRY, MOMMY. I'LL DO BETTER NEXT TIME.
I KNOW YOU WILL. YOU WANT TO MAKE IT INTO THE BIG GIRL'S STUDIO, DON'T YOU?
MORE THAN ANYTHING!
THEN WE'LL TRAIN AGAIN TOMORROW.
I'LL CANCEL OUR DINNER PLANS WITH YOUR FRIENDS, YOU'LL NEED YOUR ENERGY FOR PRACTICE.
YES, MOMMY!

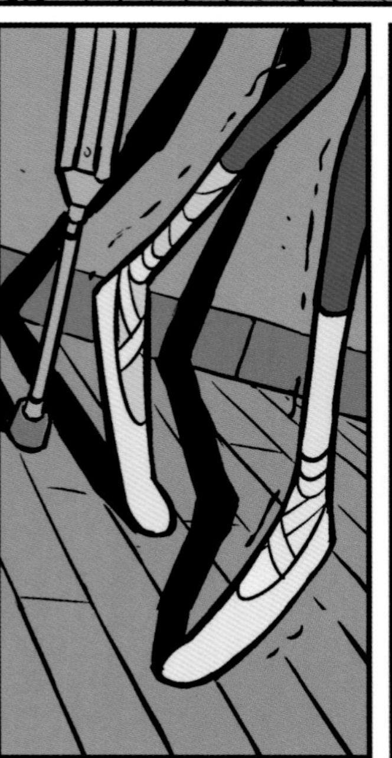

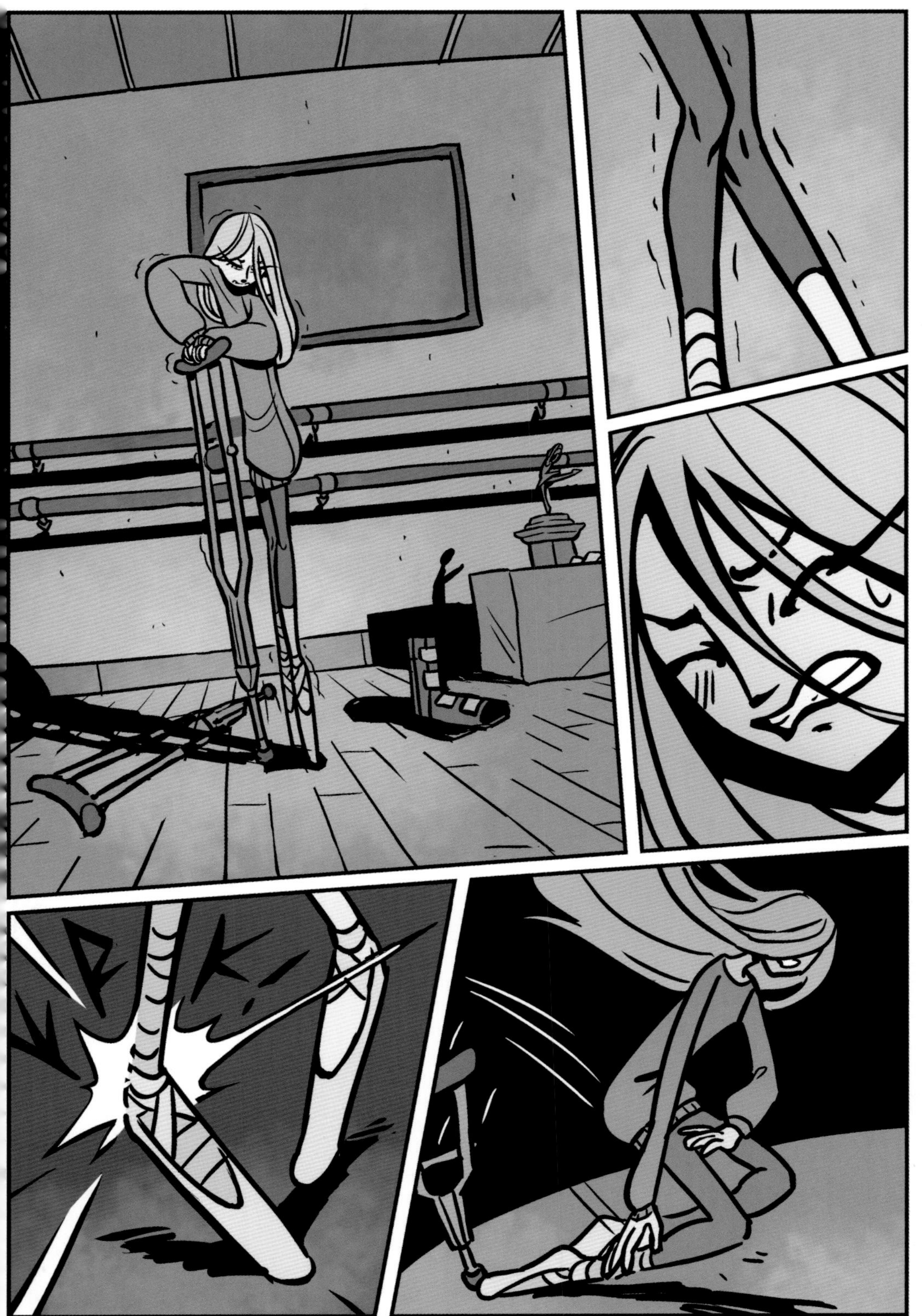

STUPID—
RAAUGH!
KSSSHH

YOU SHOULD TRY THEM ON.

WHO'S THERE?
I'M LIKE YOU, I'M NOBODY.

NO! I'M THE *PRINCIPAL* DANCER, I'M—
ARE YOU?

WEAR THESE AND YOU CAN BE SOMEBODY AGAIN.

IMPOSSIBLE...
HOW CAN THIS BE?
BECAUSE YOU WANTED IT TO.

THERE MUST BE A CATCH.

WHAT DO YOU WANT FROM ME, THEN?
EXACTLY WHAT YOU WANT: TO BE ABLE TO DANCE.

FOR YEARS I'VE WATCHED BALLERINAS FROM THIS ROOM.
I WISH TO JOIN THEM THROUGH YOU.

WEAR THESE SHOES AND SOON YOU WILL OUTPERFORM EVEN THE *PRIMA BALLERINA ASSOLUTA.*

COME BACK TOMORROW AND WE CAN BEGIN.

GOOD MORNING, DANIEL, SUZANNE.
'MORNING, MIRIAM. HOW ARE YOU FEELING TODAY?

I FEEL GREAT.
YOU LOOK FANTASTIC!

WHAT DID YOU GET UP TO LAST NIGHT?
NOTHING!

IF YOU SAY SO...

I'M GLAD TO HEAR YOU'RE FEELING BETTER, THOUGH.
THANKS.

WOAH, LOOK AT THOSE!

WHERE DID YOU GET THOSE SLIPPERS?
THEY'RE GORGEOUS!
FROM A FRIEND.

IT'S A SHAME YOU HAVE TO BREAK THEM IN. THEY'RE ALMOST TOO PRETTY TO USE!
ISN'T THAT THE FATE OF ALL POINTE SHOES?

NOW, IF YOU'LL EXCUSE ME, I HAVE SOME BUSINESS TO TAKE CARE OF.

ALEXANDRE, SIR!
I HAVE SOMETHING
TO SHOW YOU.

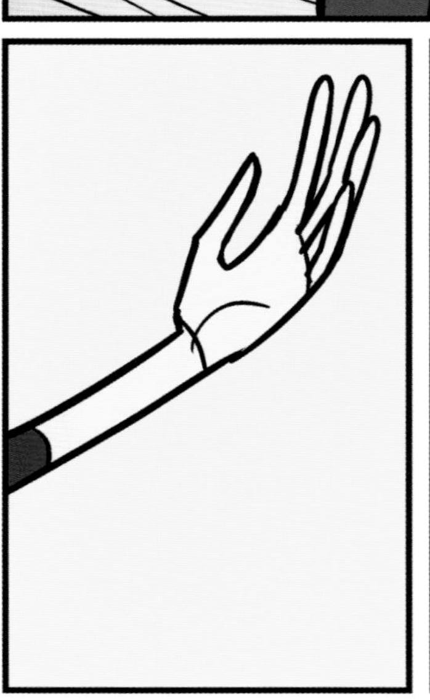

MIRIAM, THAT'S QUITE
IMPRESSIVE.

I'M GLAD TO HEAR THAT.

HOWEVER, I'M NOT SURE YOU'RE STRONG ENOUGH TO JOIN PRACTICE.

OK, LADIES, WE ARE GOING TO GO THROUGH OUR ARABESQUES.
BEGIN IN FIFTH POSITION.
NOW, PIQUÉ—
— AND FIRST ARABESQUE.
GOOD, WATCH YOUR ARMS.
NOW, SECOND ARABESQUE.
HOLD IT, LADIES.

AND INTO THIRD
MIRIAM?
DON'T TOUCH ME, I'M FINE!
I CAN DO THIS.

TAKE A SEAT, MIRIAM, YOU'RE NOT READY.
BUT, SIR—
I SAID TAKE A SEAT.

YES, SIR.

MIRIAM, I UNDERSTAND HOW MUCH YOU WANT TO GET BACK TO DANCING—
— BUT YOU MUST LOOK AFTER YOURSELF FIRST.
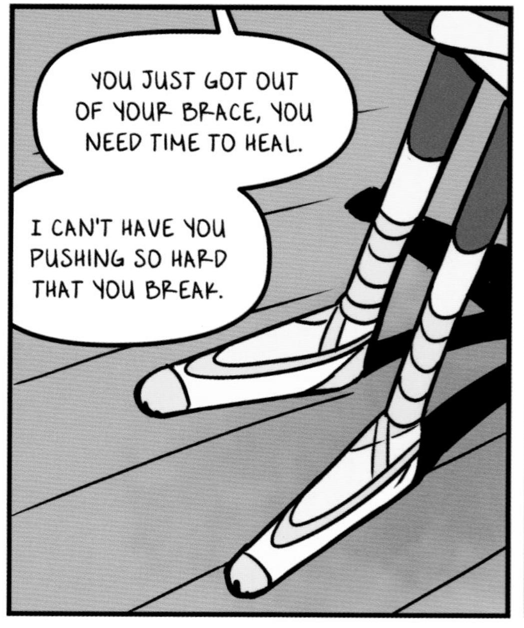
YOU JUST GOT OUT OF YOUR BRACE, YOU NEED TIME TO HEAL.
I CAN'T HAVE YOU PUSHING SO HARD THAT YOU BREAK.

IF YOU CAN GAIN YOUR STRENGTH, THERE WILL ALWAYS BE A SPOT OPEN FOR YOU IN THE CORPS.
THE CORPS?

BUT, SIR! I'M SO MUCH BETTER THAN THAT.
I'LL BE WASTED IN THE CORPS!

MIRIAM, THIS IS MY FINAL DECISION.
IT'S EITHER THE CORPS OR YOU CAN SAY GOOD-BYE TO THE BALLET.

FINE.

GOOD. NOW GET SOME REST, YOU ARE GOING TO NEED IT.

ARE YOU ALRIGHT?
I'M FINE.
GATHER AROUND, EVERYONE.

LORELEI, AS ONE OF OUR SOLOISTS, YOU'VE MADE GREAT PROGRESS IN FINESSING YOUR TECHNIQUE.

THUS, IT WOULD BE MY HONOR TO REWARD YOU FOR YOUR HARD WORK.

DANCERS–

–GIVE A ROUND OF APPLAUSE FOR YOUR NEW PRIMA BALLERINA.

3

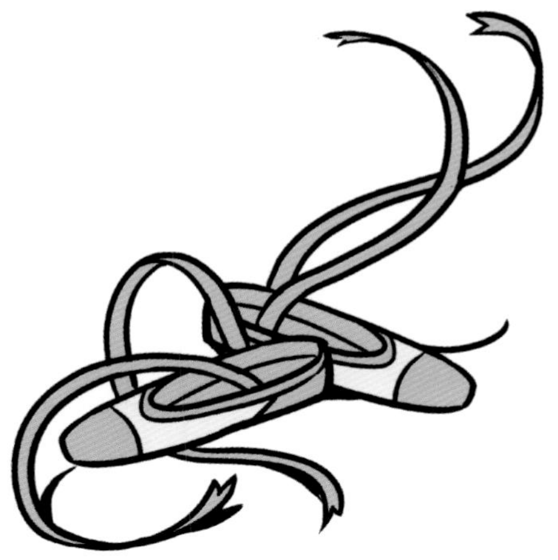

STARTING FROM THE PETITE JETÉ!
CHINS UP, EVERYONE!

DEMI-PLIÉ...
KEEP YOUR KNEES TURNED OUT!

AND JETÉ! AND AGAIN!
WATCH YOUR FEET!
MIRIAM!

TAKE FIVE EVERYONE, GET SOME WATER.
WE'LL START AGAIN AT THE PETITE JETÉ.

HEY MIRI!

MIND IF I CALL YOU THAT? MIRI?
SURE.

YOU'RE DOING GREAT SO FAR, MIRI!
WATCH YOUR BACK LEG, THOUGH, IT CAN TRIP YOU UP IF YOU'RE NOT CAREFUL.

SEE, LIKE THIS!

WHAT DOES IT MATTER?
IT'S NOT LIKE ANYONE'S GOING TO SEE US ANYWAYS.
HUH?

DON'T YOU GET IT, SUZANNE? WE'RE IN THE BALLET CORPS.
WE'RE NOBODIES.

WE'RE NOTHING MORE THAN SET DRESSING FOR THE PRINCIPAL DANCERS!
NO ONE'S GOING TO CARE WHAT WE DO.
WE'RE ONLY HERE TO MAKE LORELEI LOOK BETTER.

MIRI, THAT'S NOT FAIR.
IS THAT WHAT YOU THINK WE ARE? THE PRIMA'S BACKUP DANCERS?

I MEAN, AREN'T WE?
OH, MIRI...

BEING IN THE CORPS DE BALLET IS SO MUCH MORE THAN SPOTLIGHTING ONE DANCER.
AS DANCERS, WE SET THE TONE FOR THE WHOLE PRODUCTION.
OUR BODIES MOVE AS ONE, PAINTING EACH SCENE FOR THE AUDIENCE.
A PRIMA BALLERINA IS JUST ONE PERSON.
THE BALLET CORPS IS THE LIVING BODY THAT BREATHES LIFE INTO THE STAGE.
THOUGH, BEING PRIMA BALLERINA DOES SOUND NICE...
SUZANNE!
WHAT? A GIRL CAN DREAM!
THAT'S NOT THE POINT I'M TRYING TO MAKE.
SORRY!

MY REAL POINT IS, DON'T SELL YOURSELF SHORT.

I KNOW THINGS FEEL ROUGH SINCE EVERYTHING IS SO DIFFERENT—
—BUT REMEMBER, THIS IS SUPPOSED TO BE FUN.

BESIDES, I'M SURE WITH PRACTICE YOU'LL GET IT SOON ENOUGH.
THANKS, DANIEL.

I'M SORRY FOR SNAPPING AT YOU, SUZANNE. I THINK MY ANKLE'S ACTING UP.
DON'T SWEAT IT!

BREAK'S OVER, EVERYONE!
LET'S START AGAIN AT THE PETITE JETÉ.
THAT'S US! LET'S GO.

THAT'S IT FOR TODAY EVERYONE!
REMEMBER TO GO OVER THE CHANGES WE MADE AND BE READY FOR PRACTICE TOMORROW.

MIRIAM?

TOUGH PRACTICE TODAY, HUH?
THIS SOLO IS A LOT MORE WORK THAN I IMAGINED.
IS THAT SO?

I'M HAVING SOME TROUBLE WITH THE PAS DE DEUX THAT COMES IN LATER.

I KNOW WE HAVEN'T REACHED THAT PART OF THE DANCE YET,
— BUT I WANT TO GET AHEAD ANY WAY I CAN.

MIRIAM, COULD YOU HELP ME GO OVER IT?

I'M SORRY—
—THIS IS PROBABLY AWKWARD FOR YOU, SINCE I TOOK OVER YOUR ROLE AS PRINCIPAL DANCER...

I TOTALLY UNDERSTAND IF YOU DON'T—
I'LL DO IT.

REALLY? YOU WILL?

OF COURSE, IT'S IMPORTANT TO THE DANCE, RIGHT?

YOU'RE ALREADY SO FAR BEHIND FROM TAKING MY SPOT.
ALL EYES WILL BE ON YOU!
WE CAN'T HAVE YOU MESSING UP AND MAKING US **ALL** LOOK BAD.
OH...
I SUPPOSE THAT IS TRUE.
THANK YOU, MIRIAM. I WON'T LET YOU DOWN.

LORELEI, WATCH THAT ARM!
YOU DON'T WANT TO HIT SOMEONE IN THE FACE, DO YOU?
AH!
MIRIAM, CAN WE TAKE A BREAK? I NEED TO REST MY LEGS A SECOND.
SURE, IT'S GETTING LATE ANYWAYS.
HAAH

IS IT NIGHTTIME ALREADY?
I CAN'T BELIEVE WE'VE BEEN AT THIS FOR HOURS.
WE'RE ALMOST DONE.
WE ONLY HAVE THE LAST LEAP TO PRACTICE.
IS THAT THE ONE YOU..?
YES, THAT'S THE LEAP I FELL ON.
I'M SO SORRY.
I SWEAR I'LL DO YOU PROUD.
LET'S START AGAIN FROM THE TOP OF THE PAS DE DEUX.

CLAP!
CLAP!

LULLI DANCE

MIRIAM,
I DID IT!
WE GOT THROUGH THE
WHOLE PAS DE DEUX, I—

MIRIAM? ARE YOU ALRIGHT?

I SHOULD GO.

I DON'T KNOW WHAT KIND OF GAME YOU THINK YOU ARE PLAYING—

YOU PROMISED ME I WOULD BE STRONGER.
YOU SAID I WOULD GET MY SPOT IN THE BALLET BACK!

LOOK AT ME!
A *CORPS* DANCER!

I COULDN'T EVEN PERFORM THE SMALLEST OF JUMPS.

IT WAS HUMILIATING!
HOW IS THIS ANY BETTER THAN WHERE I WAS WITHOUT YOU?

HAS IT REALLY BEEN SO LONG?
DID YOU ALREADY FORGET?
AAUGH!

WITHOUT ME, YOU WOULD STILL BE LYING TO THE SIDE, LICKING YOUR WOUNDS.

YOUR STRENGTH WILL COME WITH TIME.
YOU ONLY NEED TO KEEP TRYING!

BUT WHERE IS THAT EXTRA BOOST YOU PROMISED ME?

HOW LONG DO YOU EXPECT ME TO WAIT—
— WHILE LORELEI MAKES HERSELF COMFORTABLE IN MY CHANGING ROOM?

SHE DOESN'T UNDERSTAND HOW HARD I WORKED TO GET HERE; THE ROLE WAS JUST *HANDED* TO HER.
NOW SHE'S DEMANDING I HELP HER CEMENT IT.

I CAN'T TAKE IT!

PATIENCE, LOVE.

I PROMISE, TOMORROW WILL BE EVEN BETTER.

LET'S GO GRAB
A DRINK, OK?

COFFEE

WHAT DID YOU WANT
TO TALK ABOUT?

NOT MUCH, I JUST
WANTED TO CHAT.

GULP
GULP

IF THAT'S ALL, WE SHOULD GET GOING. PRACTICE STARTS EARLY TOMORROW.
NO, I'M SORRY, THAT'S NOT IT.

YOU LOOK TIRED, MIRIAM. ARE YOU SLEEPING ALRIGHT?
YEAH, I'M FINE.

I THINK IT'S JUST THE AFTEREFFECTS OF MY INJURY.
I'M GETTING BETTER, BUT IT'S TOUGH.

THANK YOU FOR ASKING, THOUGH.

I'LL ALWAYS BE HERE IF YOU NEED ANYTHING.

DANIEL, TOO.
I DON'T UNDERSTAND WHY YOU TWO ARE SO NICE TO ME.

I HAVEN'T DONE ANYTHING TO DESERVE IT.

YOU DON'T HAVE TO PROVE YOURSELF FOR ME TO BE NICE TO YOU!
BUT YOU BARELY KNOW ME.

I KNOW ENOUGH TO SEE YOU'RE A GOOD PERSON—

—AND THAT'S GOTTA MEAN SOMETHING, RIGHT?

I SAW YOU HELPING LORELEI WITH HER SOLO THIS EVENING—
THAT WAS CONSIDERATE OF YOU.

THAT WAS NOTHING.
SHE'S BEHIND AFTER I LOST THE ROLE AND I DIDN'T WANT HER MAKING A FOOL OF HERSELF.

BUT YOU DIDN'T NEED TO HELP HER.
YOU COULD HAVE LEFT HER TO FIGURE IT OUT ON HER OWN.
I SUPPOSE.
DON'T SELL YOURSELF SHORT, MIRIAM.
YOU HAVE A GOOD HEART.
DON'T LET ANYONE TELL YOU OTHERWISE.

4

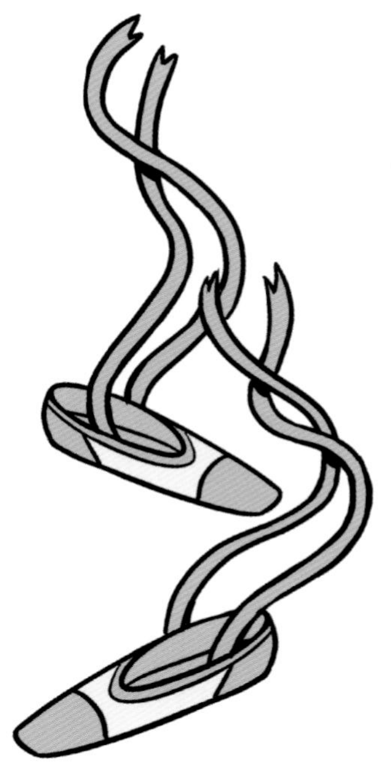

GOOD MORNING, EVERYONE!

WE'LL START TODAY WITH SOME LEAP EXERCISES, OK?
CLAP!
FINISH STRETCHING AND LINE UP!
CLAP!

REMEMBER: ONE, TWO, PLIÉ, AND JETÉ.

ALRIGHT, FIRST ROW UP!

AND FIVE, SIX, SEVEN, EIGHT!

ONE
TWO

PLIÉ, AND—

– JETÉ!
THUNK
THUMP
ACK!
HOLD ON, GROUP TWO.
LORELEI, ARE YOU OK?
YES, SIR, I'M FINE.
I'M NOT SURE WHAT CAME OVER ME...

LORELEI, DO YOU NEED TO TAKE A SECOND TO COMPOSE YOURSELF?
I'LL BE FINE, SIR, REALLY.

ALRIGHT EVERYONE, LET'S SET UP AGAIN.
FROM THE FIRST GROUP!
YES, SIR!

GOOD PRACTICE, DANCERS

SEE YOU BRIGHT AND EARLY ON MONDAY.

LORELEI, WAIT UP!

YES, MIRIAM?

THAT WAS QUITE THE FUMBLE, HUH? ARE YOU SURE YOU'RE ALRIGHT?

IT'S A BIT OVERWHELMING, ALL THIS NEW MATERIAL I'M LEARNING...

I FEEL LIKE EVERY DAY, I'M MORE AND MORE TIRED.

YOU WERE IN THIS SPOT BEFORE.
IT GETS EASIER, RIGHT?

NOT REALLY.
IF ANYTHING, I'D SAY IT ONLY GETS HARDER.
OH...

I SUPPOSE THAT IS TO BE EXPECTED WITH SUCH A STARRING ROLE...

IF YOU DON'T THINK YOU'RE CUT OUT FOR IT—

THAT'S NOT IT!

I CAN DO THIS...

AT LEAST—

— I HOPE I CAN.

THEN I'LL JUST HAVE TO KEEP PUSHING MYSELF HARDER—

— NO MATTER WHAT.

LULLI DANCE

LORELEI!
ARE YOU ALRIGHT?

YES, I AM FINE.
IT'S BEEN A LONG PRACTICE.

AAH!
LORELEI!

ALEXANDRE, SIR.

COULD I SPEAK WITH YOU PRIVATELY FOR A MOMENT?
OF COURSE, LORELEI.

POOR LORELEI...

SHE MUST HAVE BEEN WORKING HERSELF TOO HARD.
I CAN ONLY IMAGINE THE KIND OF PRESSURE SHE'S BEEN UNDER.

I GUESS SHE COULDN'T HANDLE THE STRESS.

SERIOUSLY.
I SUPPOSE "PRIMA BALLERINA" ISN'T FOR JUST ANYONE.
I DO HOPE SHE'S OK, THOUGH.

I'M SURE SHE'LL PULL THROUGH.
WHAT IS IT ABOUT BEING PRIMA THAT DESTROYS SO MUCH OF YOU?

I'M SURE YOU UNDERSTAND WHAT SHE'S GOING THROUGH THE BEST OF ALL OF US.
THE TWO OF YOU ARE SO SIMILAR...
SHE IS *NOTHING* LIKE ME.
GATHER AROUND, EVERYONE.
OH, HERE THEY COME!
WE HAVE SOME TRAGIC NEWS.

I WANTED SO BADLY TO LEAD YOU ALL—

— I DIDN'T REALIZE THE AMOUNT OF EFFORT IT WOULD TAKE.

I BELIEVE IN ALL OF YOU AND I BELIEVE IN THIS STUDIO'S SUCCESS.
THANK YOU EVERYONE—

—I'M SORRY I COULDN'T DO BETTER.
LORELEI...

THAT BEING SAID, WE'LL HAVE TO MAKE ANOTHER CHANGE TO OUR LINEUP TO FILL HER SPOT.

OUR NEW LEAD SOLOIST IS—

SUZANNE!
REALLY?
WHAT?
OH, THANK YOU SIR!
YOU HAVE NO IDEA HOW MUCH I'VE WANTED THIS.
I SWEAR I'LL DO YOU PROUD!

5

DANCE STU
THOSE SHOES...

HOW LONG HAS
IT BEEN SINCE YOU
CHANGED PAIRS?

LORELEI'S SHOES
BARELY LAST A DAY.
I HAVEN'T SEEN YOU
BREAK IN A NEW PAIR
SINCE YOU GOT THOSE...

WHAT DOES IT
MATTER TO YOU?

I CAN STILL
DANCE IN THEM.
IF YOU
SAY SO.

I TOOK LORELEI TO THE HOSPITAL.
THE LAST FEW WEEKS HAVE BEEN TEARING HER APART.

THE DOCTORS CAN'T FIGURE OUT WHAT'S WRONG WITH HER.
IT SOUNDS SERIOUS.

AND?

YOU DON'T CARE AT ALL THAT SHE'S INJURED, DO YOU?

THAT'S RICH COMING FROM YOU, NICOLAS.

I GET IT, MIRIAM. SHE TOOK YOUR PLACE AND THAT MADE YOU ANGRY.
YOU KNOW MORE ABOUT THIS THAN YOU'RE TELLING ME.

YOU STILL HAVE A RESPONSIBILITY TO THIS COMPANY—
NICOLAS, LEAVE IT.

BESIDES, WHAT DOES IT MATTER NOW?
I STILL DIDN'T GET MY ROLE BACK.

MIRIAM, LOOK AT ME.
SLAM!

WHAT, NICOLAS?
DID YOU DO SOMETHING TO LORELEI?

DON'T BE ABSURD, SHE MUST HAVE CAUGHT A COLD.

THAT THE DOCTORS COULDN'T RECOGNIZE?
WHAT KIND OF COLD LOOKS LIKE THAT?
I DON'T KNOW, I'M NOT A DOCTOR!

FINE.

MAYBE YOU HAD NOTHING TO DO WITH IT.
YOU STILL NEED TO LET THE SOLO GO.

YOUR OBSESSION ISN'T HEALTHY.
MIND YOUR OWN BUSINESS.

LIFT YOUR LEG UP!
YES, SUZANNE EXACTLY LIKE THAT.

NOW SISSONNÉ! WATCH IT...
1, 2. AND 1, 2. GOOD!

AND LEAN...
YES, SUZANNE, EXCELLENT.
NOW HERE IS WHERE THE CORPS COMES IN...

WATCH YOUR SPACING!
WE'LL END THERE, TODAY.
TOMORROW WE WILL REVIEW THE CORPS TIMING.

THAT'S IT, EVERYONE. SEE YOU BRIGHT AND EARLY TOMORROW.
MIRI!

CAN YOU BELIEVE IT?
LEAD SOLOIST...

I ALWAYS DREAMED OF GETTING HERE ONE DAY.
I DIDN'T KNOW IT WOULD BE SO SOON!
WONDERFUL.

ACTUALLY, MIRI—
— I WAS WONDERING IF YOU COULD WATCH ME AND GIVE SOME POINTERS?
WHAT?

I KNOW YOU TUTORED LORELEI BEFORE.
IT'LL BE JUST THE SAME!
FORGET ABOUT IT.

BUT, MIRIAM, ALL I NEED IS—
I SAID NO!

I'VE GIVEN SO MUCH TO THIS BALLET, AND WHAT HAVE I GOTTEN IN RETURN?
NOTHING.

SO, NO, SUZANNE.
I WON'T HELP YOU.

GO BOTHER SOMEONE ELSE ABOUT IT.

I'M DONE HELPING UNGRATEFUL PRIMAS.

FINE, DON'T HELP ME.

I'LL SEE IF LORELEI'S FEELING A LITTLE NICER.

WHAT WAS ALL THAT ABOUT?

YOU TWO GET IN A FIGHT?
IT'S NOTHING, DANIEL, JUST STAY OUT OF IT.

THAT DIDN'T SOUND LIKE NOTHING.
SUZANNE WANTED ME TO STAY BEHIND AND WATCH HER DANCE–
– I TOLD HER NO.

MIRI, I GET WHY YOU'RE UPSET, BUT IT'S NOT SUZANNE'S FAULT ALEXANDRE CHOSE HER OVER YOU.

THINGS HAPPEN, YOU'RE STILL RECOVERING FROM YOUR INJURY.

MAYBE IN THE NEXT SHOW–

WHAT, THEY'LL MAKE ME LEADER OF THE BACKGROUND DANCERS? THE NOBODIES?

DANIEL, I'M FINE NOW!
I SHOULD BE UP THERE, FRONT AND CENTER.

NOT LORELEI, NOT SUZANNE—
— ME!

MIRIAM, YOU DON'T KNOW WHAT YOU'RE SAYING...
WHATEVER, I DON'T NEED YOU PATRONIZING ME ANYWAYS.

I'M GOING TO FIX THIS MYSELF.

SPIRIT, SHOW YOURSELF!

I KNOW YOU'RE THERE.
HELLO, MIRIAM.

SPIRIT, I'VE FOLLOWED ALL OF YOUR COMMANDS WITHOUT FAIL.

I'VE WAITED AND I'VE PRACTICED, AND STILL I'M AT THE BOTTOM!
WHAT MORE DO YOU WANT?

WHAT WILL IT TAKE FOR YOU TO FINALLY GIVE ME WHAT I ASKED FOR?
OH, MY DEAR MIRIAM.

I SEE HOW MUCH YOU HAVE SUFFERED...

YOUR TIME IS COMING, THOUGH, DON'T YOU WORRY.

TELL ME, MIRIAM-

-HOW BADLY DO YOU DESIRE TO REACH THE TOP?

IT HANGS, JUST OUT OF YOUR REACH.
ARE YOU WILLING TO DO ANYTHING TO GET IT?
YES, SPIRIT!

I DON'T CARE WHAT IT TAKES.
BEING THE BEST DANCER IS ALL I'VE EVER WANTED.

ASK ME, AND I'LL DO ANYTHING!
GOOD, I'M GLAD TO HEAR THAT...

WAIT HERE.

SOON YOUR PRIZE WILL BE IN YOUR GRASP.

MIRIAM, ARE YOU STILL IN THERE?

GO AWAY, DANIEL.
I'M TIRED.
MIRI...

IF THIS IS ABOUT THE FIGHT AGAIN—
— I DON'T WANT TO TALK ABOUT IT.

NO, MIRIAM, THIS IS IMPORTANT!
IT'S SUZANNE, SHE...
SUZANNE?

SUZANNE WAS HEADING TO MEET LORELEI FOR PRACTICE—

— WHEN SHE GOT LIGHTHEADED AND COLLAPSED.
THEY WERE CROSSING THE STREET.
IT HAPPENED SO FAST...
NO...

THEY'RE IN THE AMBULANCE NOW—
— LORELEI'S FINE BUT SUZANNE'S GOING TO NEED SURGERY.

OH, MIRI, HOW COULD THIS HAVE HAPPENED?

IT'S MY FAULT...
HUH?

I DIDN'T THINK...
MIRIAM?

WHAT DID YOU DO?

beep
beep
beep
beep
beep
OH, SUZANNE...
beep
beep
beep

MIRIAM, WHAT DID YOU DO?

I *KNEW* SOMETHING WAS WRONG—
— YOU JUST CAN'T LET GO, CAN YOU?

I'M SORRY...
DID YOU PUSH HER?

COULDN'T LET HER HAVE "*YOUR TITLE*"—
— SO YOU THOUGHT YOU'D TAKE HER OUT INSTEAD?
NO! I SWEAR, I DIDN'T...

NICOLAS, THAT'S ENOUGH.

LORELEI, YOU DON'T KNOW WHAT SHE'S CAPABLE OF—
— WHAT SHE'S BEEN DOING BEHIND YOUR BACKS!

IT'S ALRIGHT.
I'LL TALK TO HER.

MIRIAM?

HI, LORELEI.
I'M GLAD YOU'RE HERE.

IT'S GOOD TO SEE YOU.
SUZANNE WOULD WANT YOU HERE.

YEAH.
SURE THING.

LORELEI, I...

I'M SORRY ABOUT SUZANNE.
WHAT ARE YOU APOLOGIZING FOR?

I WAS THERE–
– NO MATTER WHAT NICOLAS SAYS, I KNOW YOU DIDN'T PUSH HER.
NO, BUT I...

I FEEL LIKE I MIGHT AS WELL HAVE.
WHAT DO YOU MEAN?

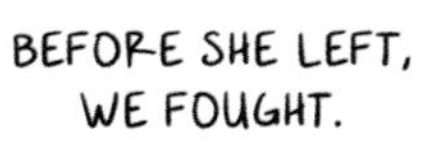
BEFORE SHE LEFT, WE FOUGHT.

I'D BEEN ANGRY AT HER SINCE SHE WAS PROMOTED.
I SAID SO MANY HORRIBLE THINGS TO HER...

IT SOUNDS TERRIBLE–
– BUT I WANTED HER TO FAIL, NO MATTER WHAT...

I NEVER IMAGINED SOMETHING LIKE THIS HAPPENING...

BUT, I WASN'T A GOOD FRIEND TO HER EITHER.

YOU TOO.
I COULDN'T GET OVER MYSELF AND JUST BE HAPPY FOR YOU WHEN YOU GOT YOUR TURN.

NICOLAS TOLD ME ABOUT YOUR HOSPITAL VISIT.

EVER SINCE MY OWN ACCIDENT AND LOSING MY SOLO—
— YOU'VE BEEN GETTING MORE AND MORE EXHAUSTED.

I SHOULD HAVE SAID SOMETHING SOONER.

MIRIAM, I'M SORRY YOU LOST YOUR SOLO—
— BUT IT GAVE ME THE OPPORTUNITY I NEEDED TO SHOW MY WORTH.

I'VE ALWAYS WANTED TO BE PRIMA BALLERINA, EVER SINCE I WAS YOUNG.
WHEN I FINALLY GOT MY TURN TO PROVE I DESERVED IT—
— I PUSHED MYSELF TO MY LIMITS, PRACTICING AND TRAINING.

I WORKED MYSELF TOO HARD...

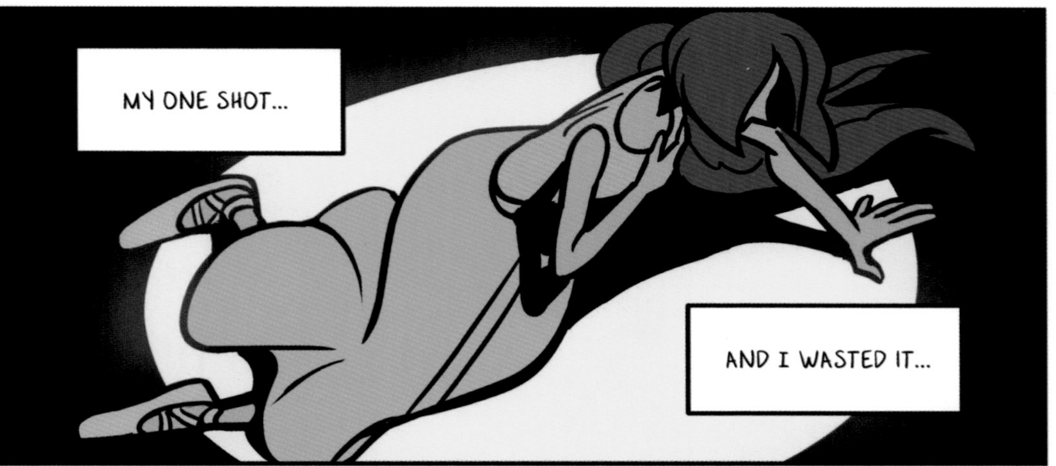
MY ONE SHOT...
AND I WASTED IT...

IF I HAD JUST DONE MY JOB, SUZANNE WOULDN'T HAVE HAD TO OVERWORK HERSELF.
SHE WOULDN'T HAVE COLLAPSED!

IT'S ALL...
MY FAULT...

SHH, LORELEI—
— IT'S OK...

I'M SORRY LORELEI.
I DIDN'T REALIZE...

I'M SO SORRY...

LULLI DANCE ST

I'M GOING TO MAKE THIS RIGHT.

6

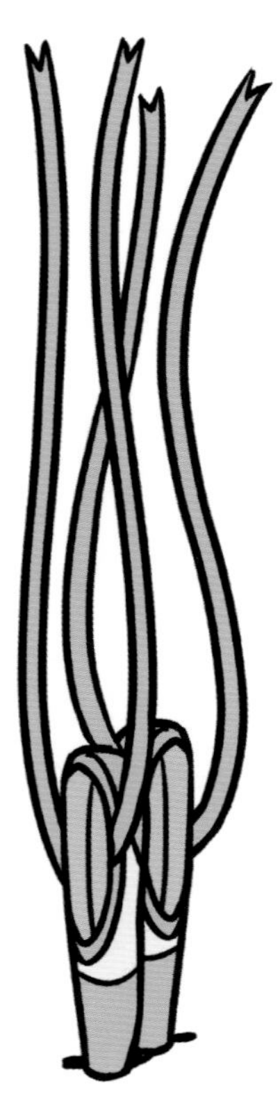

SPIRIT, WHERE ARE YOU?

SHOW YOURSELF!

I AM HERE, LOVE.

SPIRIT, WHAT HAVE YOU DONE?

EVERYTHING IS ALL WRONG!

I DON'T UNDERSTAND, ISN'T THIS WHAT YOU WANTED?
ALL YOU'VE DONE IS CAUSE PAIN!

SUZANNE'S IN THE HOSPITAL...
SHE COULD HAVE DIED!

BUT YOU'RE STRONGER NOW, AREN'T YOU?
WHAT?

FOR WEEKS YOU'VE BEEN DRAWING FROM LORELEI'S ABILITIES.

BUT LORELEI WASN'T—
-YOUR FRIEND?

YOU'RE RIGHT.

I WAS UPSET—
— BUT I NEVER SHOULD HAVE TRIED TO HURT HER EITHER.

YOU ASKED FOR THE STRENGTH TO DANCE AGAIN, AND I GAVE IT TO YOU.

FOR THESE LAST FEW WEEKS I'VE BEEN ALIVE ON THE STAGE!
I'VE GIVEN YOU EVERYTHING YOU COULD HAVE EVER HOPED FOR!
YOUR POISE, YOUR FINESSE...
YOU OWE EVERYTHING YOU ARE TO ME.

WHO CARES IF WE HAVE TO TAKE DOWN A FEW OTHER GIRLS TO GET TO THE TOP?
ISN'T THAT ONLY FAIR?

FAIR?
HOW COULD THAT POSSIBLY BE FAIR?

I CAN'T HELP YOU DESTROY OTHER PEOPLE'S LIVES...

OUR DEAL IS OFF.
WHAT?

YOU'RE GOING TO GIVE UP *EVERYTHING* WE'VE WORKED FOR BECAUSE WE WERE THE ONLY ONES *DETERMINED* ENOUGH TO TAKE IT?

I'M DONE WITH YOU, SPIRIT.

AND I'M DONE WITH THESE SHOES.

NO!!

WHAT?

SPIRIT, WHAT IS THE MEANING OF THIS?
I WON'T LET YOU DESTROY ALL THAT I'VE EARNED...

YOU'RE MINE, MIRIAM!
YOUR EVERY MOVE-
- YOUR EVERY BREATH!
MINE!!

AAUGH!

NO!
WHAT ARE YOU DOING, MIRIAM?
JUST GIVE IN!
WE CAN GO BACK TO EXACTLY AS WE WERE...
RAUGH!

SPIRIT, ENOUGH!
I WON'T LET YOU OVERTAKE ME!
I'M ENDING THIS!

NO!
STOP!
STOP IT!
PLEASE...

NO!
IT'S NOT FAIR!
NONE OF THIS IS FAIR...
SPIRIT...
I'M SORRY—
—BUT I REFUSE TO BE LIKE YOU ANYMORE.

HURTING YOU, HURTING MY FRIENDS...
I CAN'T LET THIS BECOME WHO I AM.
DON'T YOU SEE?
OH, BUT MIRIAM, YOU *ARE* JUST LIKE ME.
WE'RE ONE AND THE SAME...

WHAT A CUTE LITTLE GIRL!
NOT VERY TALENTED, THOUGH, IS SHE?

HA! HA!
HA! HA! HA!
HA! HA! HA!
HA! HA! HA!

MOMMY!
OH, SWEETIE.
EVERYONE HATED IT!
I MESSED UP EVERYTHING!
HONEY, IT'S OK...
JUST BREATHE...
WE'RE JUST GONNA HAVE TO TRY HARDER NEXT TIME, OK?
OK...
WE'RE GONNA SHOW THOSE OTHER KIDS WHAT YOU'RE REALLY MADE OF
YOU WANNA BE THE BEST, RIGHT?
YES!

THEN WE'RE JUST GONNA
HAVE TO PUSH HARDER UNTIL
YOU REACH THE TOP.

IT'S OK, MIRIAM. YOU STILL HAVE YOUR DANCING.
YEAH...
REPORT

SEE, MIRIAM?
I'VE ONLY EVER WANTED EXACTLY WHAT YOU WANT.

IT'S NOT FAIR THAT THESE OTHER GIRLS GET TO HAVE WHAT YOU'VE WORKED SO HARD TO ACHIEVE.

IT'S ONLY RIGHT THAT WE GET TO TAKE IT BACK!

THE PRIMA BALLERINA TITLE IS OURS!
WE'RE SO MUCH BETTER THAN LORELEI... THAN SUZANNE...

WHAT DID THEY EVER DO TO DESERVE THAT HONOR?
SPIRIT, IT'S ALRIGHT, YOU CAN STOP NOW.
I UNDERSTAND.
I KNOW HOW HARD WE WORKED TO GET TO THIS STAGE—
— HOW MUCH WE BLED FOR THIS.
BUT LIFE ISN'T ALWAYS FAIR.
WE CAN'T LASH OUT AT OTHER PEOPLE FOR THE BAD HAND WE'VE BEEN DEALT.
LORELEI, SUZANNE... I'VE SEEN HOW BADLY THEY WANT THE TITLE.
JUST BECAUSE I'VE BLED FOR IT DOESN'T MEAN THEY HAVEN'T, TOO!

WE'VE ALL FELT PAIN.
I CAN'T USE MINE TO TEAR THEM DOWN.

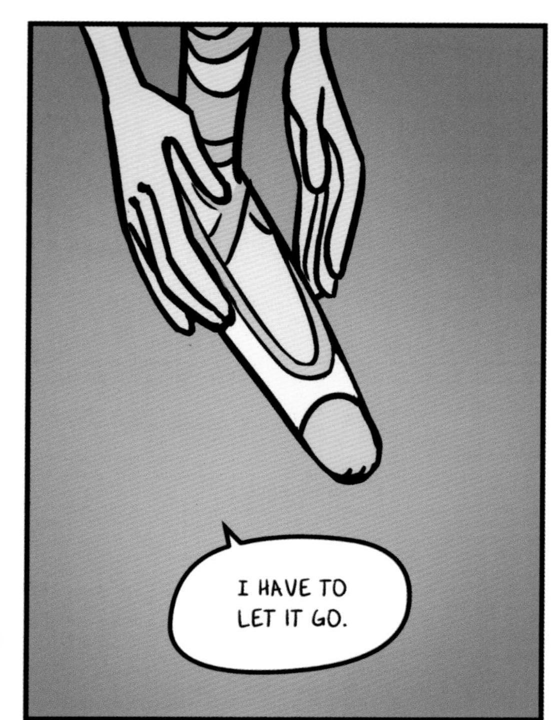
I HAVE TO LET IT GO.

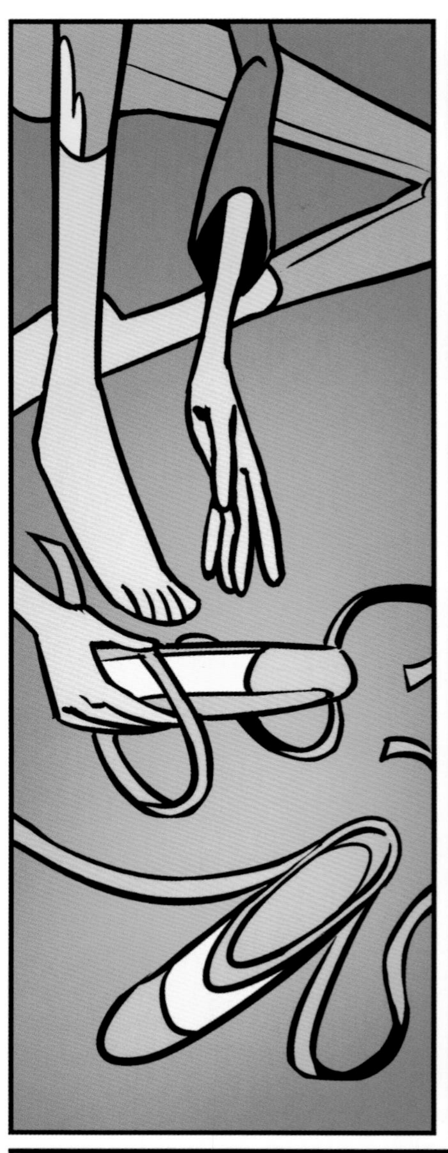

MAYBE NOW—
—WE CAN FINALLY HEAL.

STILL, THANK YOU–

– FOR GIVING ME ANOTHER CHANCE.

7

KNOCK KNOCK?

DANIEL, SUZANNE—
IT'S NICE TO SEE YOU.

WHEN DID YOU GET OUT OF THE HOSPITAL, SUZANNE?
YESTERDAY! YOU'VE BEEN OUT FOR A LITTLE WHILE.

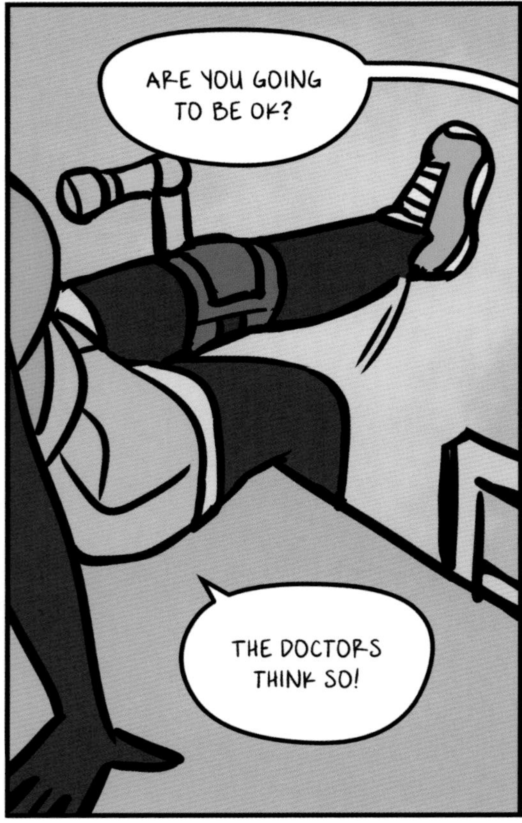
ARE YOU GOING TO BE OK?
THE DOCTORS THINK SO!

I'LL NEED A BIT OF PHYSICAL THERAPY—
— BUT IN A COUPLE WEEKS I SHOULD BE GOOD AS NEW.
THAT'S A RELIEF.

WHAT ABOUT YOU?
HOW ARE YOU FEELING, MIRI?

HONESTLY? BETTER THAN I HAVE IN WEEKS.

WHAT HAPPENED TO YOUR LEG?

I DON'T KNOW THAT IT EVER REALLY HEALED PROPERLY, BEFORE.

SUZANNE, I'M SORRY FOR SNAPPING AT YOU EARLIER.

YOU WERE THOUGHTFUL ENOUGH TO ASK FOR HELP–
– AND INSTEAD OF JUST SAYING "NO" I LASHED OUT AGAINST YOU.

YOU DESERVED BETTER THAN THAT.
CAN YOU FORGIVE ME?
I MEAN, YOU WERE BEING A TOTAL JERK...

HEY, I'M APOLOGIZING!
YOU COULD BE A LITTLE NICER–
MIRI...

SORRY...

I'M STILL WORKING ON IT.

BUT, YEAH, I CAN FORGIVE YOU.
WE'RE FRIENDS AFTER ALL, RIGHT?
YEAH, FRIENDS.
THANK YOU, SUZANNE.

YOU TOO, DANIEL.
I'M SORRY FOR ALWAYS PUSHING YOU AWAY, I KNOW YOU CARE ABOUT ME.

THANK YOU FOR THAT.
IT'S NO WORRY.

SUZANNE, AS SOON AS YOU'RE DONE WITH THERAPY, I WOULD LOVE TO HELP YOU WITH YOUR SOLO.

I'D LIKE THAT.

OH, MIRI!
THE DOCTOR CAME BY EARLIER, WHILE YOU WERE ASLEEP.
GET WELL SOON

SHE SAID YOUR LEG IS LOOKING MUCH BETTER THAN THE LAST TIME YOU CAME IN.
ISN'T THAT GREAT?
REALLY?

YEAH!
AT THIS RATE, YOU SHOULD BE ABLE TO COME BACK TO THE STUDIO IN NO TIME!

I THINK I'LL TRY TEACHING.

MISS YOU!

LOOK AT THE TIME!
WE SHOULD GET GOING IF YOU WANT TO GET ANY PRACTICE IN TONIGHT, DANIEL.
IT WAS GREAT TALKING TO YOU, MIRI.
LET US KNOW WHEN YOU GET OUT AND WE'LL CELEBRATE!
SOUNDS LIKE A PLAN.
SEE YOU LATER!
DON'T BE SCARED, SPIRIT.
YOU CAN COME OUT NOW.

THINGS ARE GOING TO BE DIFFERENT NOW, OK?
IT'S GOING TO HURT, GIVING UP THE STAGE—
—BUT IT'S FOR THE BEST.
BUT WHAT ABOUT OUR DREAM?
DREAMS CHANGE, WE SET NEW GOALS.
I THINK IF I TAKE UP COACHING, I CAN HELP OTHER CHILDREN SO THEY DON'T END UP LIKE ME—
— LIKE US.

THANK YOU–

– I'LL LOOK FORWARD TO IT.

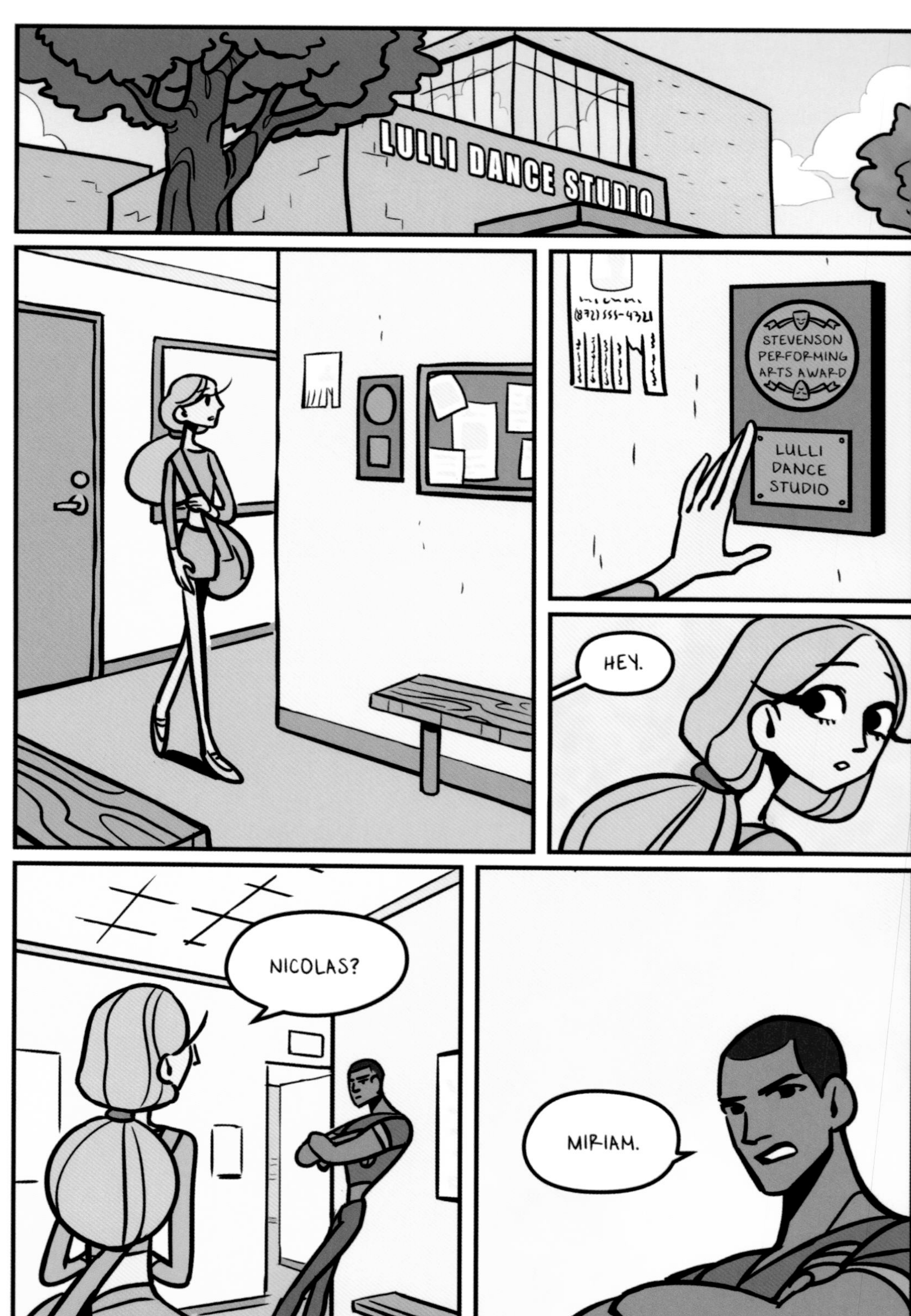
LULLI DANCE STUDIO
(872) 555-4321
STEVENSON PERFORMING ARTS AWARD
LULLI DANCE STUDIO
HEY.
NICOLAS?
MIRIAM.

WHAT DO YOU WANT?

HAVE YOU SEEN LORELEI?

WHY?

I PROMISE, I DON'T MEAN HER ANY HARM.

I JUST WANT TO TALK.

NICOLAS, I'M SORRY FOR EVERYTHING THAT HAPPENED.

THINGS GOT OUT OF CONTROL—
— AND I LET MY OBSESSION WITH MY ROLE GET THE BEST OF ME.

HONESTLY, MIRIAM, I DON'T CARE WHAT YOU DID OR DIDN'T DO.
LORELEI AND SUZANNE ARE OK NOW AND THAT'S ALL THAT MATTERS.

THAT DOESN'T MEAN I'M GOING TO FORGIVE YOU, THOUGH.
I DON'T EXPECT YOU TO.

SHE'S IN THERE, PRACTICING.

DON'T PULL ANYTHING FUNNY.

THANK YOU, NICOLAS.
I'LL BE QUICK.

GOOD LUCK IN THE FUTURE.
YOU TOO.

HEY, LORELEI.
MIRIAM!
COME SIT WITH ME!
THANKS.
CONGRATULATIONS ON THE SPEEDY RECOVERY.

THANK YOU, MIRIAM.
I'VE BEEN SEEING A PHYSICAL THERAPIST.

HE SAYS I'M JUST ABOUT READY TO GET BACK ON STAGE.

YOU'VE REALLY COME A LONG WAY.
WE BOTH HAVE.

SO, WHAT BRINGS YOU OUT HERE?

LORELEI...

I...
DANCE WITH ME?

WHAT?
RIGHT NOW?

DANCING HAS ALWAYS HELPED ME WORK THROUGH MY THOUGHTS.

SO, WILL YOU DANCE WITH ME?

OK.

I WANTED TO SAY SORRY FOR THE WAY I ACTED AROUND YOU.
I WAS JEALOUS—
— SEEING YOU SUCCEED WHERE I FAILED.
I'M TRYING TO BE A BETTER PERSON NOW...
BUT OLD HABITS DIE HARD—
— YOU KNOW?
YES, I DO.

I THOUGHT THAT, MAYBE—
— NOW THAT I'M NOT WITH THE TROUPE ANYMORE...

MAYBE WE COULD BE FRIENDS?
MIRIAM, I WOULD LOVE NOTHING MORE.

LORELEI, GOOD LUCK WITH THIS AUDITION SEASON.

THANK YOU.
I DO HOPE YOU CAN LAND ANOTHER PRINCIPAL SOLO.
YOU DESERVE IT.

I HEAR YOU'VE STARTED TEACHING YOUR OWN LESSONS.
HOW IS THAT GOING?
IT'S TOUGH, BUT IT'S GOOD WORK.
I KNOW THAT I WON'T EVER BE STRONG ENOUGH TO DANCE ON THE STAGE AGAIN—
— BUT I'M GLAD I DON'T HAVE TO GIVE UP DANCING ENTIRELY.
THEY'RE GOOD KIDS, TOO.
WATCH OUT, LORELEI.
ONE OF THEM MIGHT TAKE YOUR PLACE SOME DAY.
THEY ALL HAVE SO MUCH POTENTIAL—
— I ONLY HOPE I CAN BE A GOOD INFLUENCE ON THEM.

AND FIRST POSITION, FIVE, SIX, SEVEN, EIGHT.
TENDU FORWARD AND CLOSE.
TENDU SIDE AND CLOSE.
TENDU BACK AND CLOSE.
PLIÉ AND AGAIN!
FRONT AND CLOSE.
SIDE AND CLOSE.
KEEP YOUR ARMS RAISED!
ACK!
EVERYONE, TAKE A BREAK.
GOOD WORK SO FAR!
HI, EMILY. HOW ARE YOU DOING?

YOU KNOW, IT'S OK TO MESS UP.

I CAN'T GET IT RIGHT...
DOES THAT BOTHER YOU?

I WANNA BE IN THE BIG KIDS' CLASS!
I NEED TO BE THE BEST.

NOT EVERYONE IS GOING TO GET IT THE FIRST TIME, OR THE SECOND TIME.
DON'T PUSH YOURSELF TOO HARD.

BUT CARRIE AND AUSTIN ALREADY MADE IT TO THE BIG KIDS' CLASS!
THEY'RE GOING TO LEAVE ME BEHIND...

IT'S NOT ABOUT BEING THE BEST.
I WANT YOU TO HAVE FUN HERE!
DON'T WORRY ABOUT ANY OF THE OTHER KIDS.
YOUR FRIENDS LOVE YOU, NO MATTER WHICH CLASS YOU'RE IN.
YOU'LL ALWAYS HAVE SCHOOL AND AFTER PRACTICE TO HANG OUT WITH CARRIE AND AUSTIN.
FOR NOW, LET'S FOCUS ON DOING WHAT MAKES YOU HAPPY.
YES, MS. MIRIAM!
GOOD, NOW GO, TAKE YOUR BREAK.
WE'LL START AGAIN WITH THE TENDUS SOON.
OK!

About the Author

Hanna Schroy is a cartoonist and illustrator living in Austin. She has participated in a multitude of self-published anthologies including *Girls! Girls! Girls!*, curated by Alex Perkins, and *Thicker Than Blood*, curated by Mengmeng Liu. She is a long-time dance enthusiast and recent amateur gardener. hannaschroy.com

Acknowledgements

Thank you to Mom, Dad, Aunt Becca, Mimi, and Papa for giving me the chance to dance for 15 years. Your support inspired me not only to dance but to draw and explore new creative outlets even when I didn't believe in myself. Thank you for everything you've given me that has gotten me to this point, I hope I've done you proud.

Thank you to my editor Andrea for putting your faith in me and encouraging me every step of the way. Thank you to Spike for giving me the chance to make this happen.

Thank you to Ally Schroy, Caitlin Scannell, David Pender, Maggie Kelner, and Jae Lin for all of the work you did, helping me review my drafts, flat my pages, and so much more. When everything became overwhelming, you all pulled me to the finish line. I could not have completed this book without you.

Glossary of Ballet Terms

Arabesques *(air-uh-besk)* – French for "in Arabic fashion." A pose where the dancer is standing on one leg with their other leg extended straight behind them.

Ballet Company – A dance troupe that performs ballet, a type of dance that originated in Europe. Many ballet companies also have schools to train dancers.

Ballet Master/Ballet Mistress – A person in charge of running dance classes and rehearsals for a ballet company.

Barre *(bar)* – A horizontal bar that is in ballet rehearsal rooms. A dancer will hold lightly onto the barre for additional support while doing warm ups.

Corps de ballet *(core-duh-ba-lay)* – French for "body of the ballet." Members of the corps are the lowest rank of dancers in a ballet company. They dance with synchronized movements and are used as a background for the principal dancers.

Chassé *(sha-say)* – French for "to chase." A dance step where the dancer extends one foot forward and the back foot meets up with it before the front foot shoots forward again. This looks like the back foot is chasing the front foot.

Choreography – The sequence of steps and patterns put together that make up the ballet or dance.

Demi-plié *(dem-ee-plee-ey)* – French for "half bend" A movement where the dancer stands in one of the five positions and bends their knees while keeping their heels on the ground.

Fifth Position – The last of the five fundamental poses for ballet dancers. A pose where the dancer stands with their feet turned out and the front foot's heel touches the back foot's toe while the back foot's heel touches the front foot's toe.

First Position – The first of the five fundamental poses for ballet dancers. A pose where the dancer sets their heels together and turns their toes out so that their feet are in a straight line.

Fourth Position – A pose where the dancer has their toes pointed out and one foot is set slightly in front of the other.

Jeté *(juh-tay)* – French for "thrown." A jump where the dancer jumps from one foot and lands on the other. A Petite Jeté is a small jump and a Grand Jeté is a larger jump.

Pas de Bourrée *(pah-dey-boo-rey)* – French for "beating steps." A move where the dancer steps sideways, passing one foot in front of the other.

Pas de deux *(pah-dey-doo)* – French for "step of two." A dance where two dancers, typically done by a pair of principal dancers, perform steps together. This is often a romantic moment between characters in a ballet.

Piqué *(pee-kay)* – French for "pricking." A dance move where a dancer transfers weight onto one leg on full pointe, also known as "piqué sur la pointe." From here a dancer can move to a pirouette.

Pirouette *(peer-oh-et)* – French for "spin." A move where the dancer is balancing on one foot while spinning in a circle.

Plié *(plee-ay)* – French for "to bend." A move where the dancer has their feet turned out, their heels on the ground, and bends their knees.

Pointe *(point)* – A technique in classical ballet where the dancer supports all their body weight on the tips of their toes while dancing, also called "en pointe." They are aided by pointe shoes, which wear out quickly and are replaced often.

Prima Ballerina *(pree-ma ba-luh-ree-nah)* – Italian for "first dancer." The highest ranking female dancer in a ballet company.

Prima Ballerina Assoluta *(pree-ma ba-luh-ree-nah a-seh-loo-ta)* – Italian for "absolute first dancer." The rare title is awarded to the most prestigious of female ballet dancers. It is a rank even higher than Principal and Prima Ballerina and is an honor bestowed on only a few dancers every generation.

Principal Dancer – The highest rank of dancer in a ballet company. These dancers are the stars of ballet productions and play lead roles.

Relevé *(re-luh-vay)* – French for "raised." A movement where the ballet dancer rises up and stands on their toes or "en pointe."

Second Position – A pose where the dancer has their feet spread apart with feet turned out.

Soloist – A dancer who is a level above the corp de ballet but below principal dancer. These dancers often perform solo dances and play supporting characters in a story ballet. A First Soloist is a dancer being considered for promotion to Principal.

Tendu *(ten-doo)* – French for "tight" A move where the dancer has one leg stretched away from their body and the toe of the extended leg still touches the ground.

Third Position – A pose where the dancer has one foot in front of the other. The heel of the front foot is touching the arch of the back foot.

Concept Art